D0070453

2007 – 2008

Donated to the
Prairie Vista Birthday
Book Club

by

Evan Hosinski
July 25th

An anthology of short stories by

Joseph Bruchac

David Lubar

Marilyn Singer

Terry Trueman

Dorian Cirrone

Tanya West

Alexandra Siy

Jamie McEwan

Edited by Tanya Dean

Cataloging-in-Publication

Sports shorts : an anthology of short stories / by Joseph Bruchac ... [et al].
p. ; cm.
ISBN-13: 978-1-58196-040-2 Trade hardcover
ISBN-10: 1-58196-040-9 Trade hardcover
ISBN-13: 978-1-58196-058-7 Trade paperback
ISBN-10: 1-58196-058-1 Trade paperback

Summary: A collection of eight semi-autobiographical stories about the authors' experiences with sports while growing up. They range from the game "Bombardment" over the lunch hour, sports from gym class, karate, ballet, and wrestling, to baseball, basketball and football. — Contents: Bombardment / Joseph Bruchac — Two left feet, two left hands, and too left on the bench / David Lubar — First position / Marilyn Singer — Finishing blocks and deadly hook shots / Terry Trueman — Finding high-jump fame / Dorian Cirrone — Line drive / Tanya West — Riding the century / Alexandra Siy — On being written in / Jamie McEwan.
1. Sports — Juvenile fiction. 2. Athletic ability — Juvenile fiction. 3. Sportsmanship — Juvenile fiction. [1. Sports — Fiction. 2. Athletic ability — Fiction. 3. Sportsmanship — Fiction. 4. Short stories.] I. Title. II. Author.
PS648.S78 S667 2005
813/.0108357 dc22
OCLC: 58434746

Published by Darby Creek Publishing,
A division of Oxford Resources, Inc.
7858 Industrial Parkway
Plain City, OH 43064
www.darbycreekpublishing.com

Printed in the United States of America

2 4 6 8 10 9 7 5 3

CONTENTS

Bombardment

by

Joseph Bruchac

"READY?"

Coach Fasulo held the three volleyballs cupped in his big hands like a juggler about to begin his act. But that was not what was going to happen. Far from it. And right now those volleyballs were not just volleyballs. They were ammunition.

"SET?"

A hundred pairs of eyes watched intently from the two ends of the gym. Some were fearful, some eager as wolves waiting for the first rabbit to show itself, some uncertain of whether they were predator or prey. I was pretty sure of what I was, though. My role was as set in my own mind as it was in the minds of all the other boys who were invariably a head taller than I. I was fresh meat.

I hadn't joined those who managed to manufacture some lame excuse so they could sit it out on the bleachers below the five-high, arched, screen-protected windows on the north side of the old Saratoga High School on Lake Avenue.

I gotta cold.

Turned my ankle.

I don't feel so good, Coach.

I broke my fingernail.

My own imagination was more fertile than that. I'd memorized from my grandmother's unabridged dictionary at least one major disease or debilitating condition for every letter of the alphabet from "arthritis" to "zoophobia." But I never took the easy way out—even though I knew I'd be an easy out whenever I caught the eye of one of the big boys on the other side who knew a soft target when he saw one. Even though I'd had three pairs of glasses broken, had suffered two bloody noses, and had the wind knocked out of me a dozen times over the last year, I needed to be out there. A part of me felt like a lemming following its fellows over the cliff into the Arctic Ocean, but I couldn't resist.

When noon recess came and we were given the option to go to the gym, I always trotted so fast down the hall on my little doomed feet that I was often the first to step out on the wooden floor where combat would soon ensue.

"GO!"

Coach Fasulo tossed the balls up and back-pedaled for the safety of the sidelines as the bravest or most foolhardy players on each side leapt forward to grab those dangerous globes that glistened like three spinning full moons.

Red, a lanky, long-armed kid who was also a baseball pitcher, caught one of the white spheres one-handed and hurled it at our side.

WHOMP!

Red's shot nailed a chunky kid. I didn't know his name, but he'd had the misfortune of stepping in front of me just then. He was hit so hard that he fell to his knees holding his stomach and then crawled to the bleachers.

I should have sympathized with him, but I was too exultant. That ball had been meant for me. Bombardment had begun, and, for once, I wasn't the first man out.

KA-THOMP! WHAP! THUNK!

The three balls that hit in rapid succession, taking my feet out from under me, spinning me around, and bloodying my lower lip made it painfully clear that I was, however, the second.

Bombardment. The way it was played and the rules of the game could not have been simpler. Imagine a typical school gym. Take a group of kids—ten, twenty, a hundred—and divide them into two equal sides. The line in the middle of the court splits the two territories. Step over that line, and you're a goner, banished to the bleachers with other early failures of survival of the fittest.

The laws of nature had nothing on Bombardment when it came to the pitilessness of the three ways you were eliminated from play.

Step over the line. Out.

Get hit clean (not on the bounce) by a ball from the other side. Out.

Throw the ball and have it caught by your victim. Out.

It didn't matter how much I loved that game—I was always the last one chosen. I was different from the other kids. (I know now that every kid is different from all the other kids. Even the kids whom I'd thought "had it made in the shade" had their own hard rows to hoe—as Grampa Jesse used to put it. But I didn't understand that back then.)

I was different because I was being raised by my grandparents. All of the other kids I went to school with lived with their parents. Their dads went to work eight hours a day from nine to five. Their moms stayed home and took care of their families. My grandparents, who ran a little general store, were always home. My grandmother, the head of our family, was an intellectual who'd graduated from Albany Law School and passed the bar, but never practiced. My dark-skinned grandfather had left school in fourth grade, jumping out the window when they called him a dirty Indian one too many times. My grandparents had met while Grampa was working as a hired man for Grama's father. Their marriage had been, to put it lightly, a scandal.

None of that was as important to me. Our home in rural Greenfield was miles away from Saratoga. I read my grandmother's books, helped out at the store, and spent the rest of my free time in the woods. In town, kids got together to play games and learn how to get along.

I didn't know how to pass or catch or block or dribble or swing or tackle. Instead of the names, numbers, and stats of sports heroes, I knew the plots of great books and could recite long poems by heart. Big deal.

Other personal details seemed inexorably destined to bar me forever from organized sports. One—already mentioned but worth repeating—was that I was knee-high to a gopher. Kids joked about my being so small they had to look twice to see me. The next was the big mouth I'd developed as a way of compensating for my dearth of physical visibility. I collected my share of bruises from bigger kids who became irked when

I made such observations as "Your excessive reliance on brute force borders on psychosis."

The biggest obstacle, though, was not me. It was Grama.

Grampa had never played sports himself. By the age of nine, he'd been working in the woods with the men. He'd tried to toss a ball with me, but his age was such that all I had to do was throw one a little too high and it would go sailing by him like he was made of wood. Much as I loved him, a wall was better at pitch-and-catch than Grampa. If it had just been up to him, he'd have gladly let me stay after school to play sports.

Grama, though, ruled the roost. In her grim determination to shield me from harm, she was more protective than a mother bird. She wouldn't even let me ride the bus. She drove me in, watching like a hawk until I was safely inside the door. At the end of each school day, I'd find her waiting, eagle-eyed and ten minutes early, in her old blue Plymouth.

Even worse, she'd made a point of cautioning Coach Fasulo about my fragility. "Keep a special eye on my boy, Sonny, during gym."

She'd spoken to *all* of my teachers—and to the parents of any kid she'd learned had laid a hand on me. Did I mention that my grandmother was also a member of the school board?

"That Marion Bowman," I once overheard my homeroom teacher say, "is a force of nature."

I understood what Mrs. Hall meant. If the National Weather Service had observed my grandmother acting in my defense, it would have named every hurricane after her.

To Coach Fasulo's credit, even though he nodded—seemingly in agreement with Grama's dictates, he never kept me from attempting (and usually failing) any of the really dangerous things we did in gym class, from the climb up the long rope to the ceiling fifty feet above (I managed a pitiful eight feet in ascent) to bouncing off the springboard into a flawed front flip that ended with me on my back, gasping like a beached bass. Even something as simple as a forward roll was beyond my bungling ability, concluding not on my feet, but with my face planted in the canvas mat that smelled like five generations of dirty sweat socks. But I kept trying.

How easy it is to close my eyes and see Coach Fasulo and remember the totally uncondescending way he treated the undergrown, inept, and suicidally eager kid I was then. Did he realize that whenever he walked down the hall with those three volleyballs in his hands and saw me waiting outside the gym and said, "Ready to go, Bruchac?" that those few words were as much of an inspiration to me as Prince Hal's speech to the battleworn English troops on St. Crispin's Day?

Bombardment, with its simple, violent, semi-controlled chaos, was my only release. Fortunately, Grama never heard of it. As far as she knew, I spent my lunch hour carefully chewing every bite fifty times while memorizing Shakespeare.

I don't know how many times I played Bombardment. However many, it wasn't nearly enough. If I could have rewritten the myth of Sisyphus, the man condemned by the Greek gods to forever push a stone up a hill, to give that story a happy ending, I would have had him eternally in the midst of a game of Bombardment. And not just any game—but the one that I remember more than any other.

Until the lunch hour, it had been a school day like most others. Ditto for the menu. Stacks of stale bread, globs of tuna surprise, little cups of fruit cocktail, and luminous blocks of unsweetened green Jell-O. I wolfed down what was plopped on my plastic plate and then legged it for the gym.

I wasn't the first one there. A dozen kids were already gathered around Coach Fasulo, and more were arriving in a steady stream. Football was the most popular spectator sport after school, but our mid-day mayhem attracted almost as enthusiastic a crowd. That day, it looked as if we were going to break a record. There was no real reason for it. It wasn't raining outside, and there was no major rivalry to watch, where sides were set ahead of time. It was all random—it just happened.

And it just happened that, for the first time, when Coach Fasulo reached out to put his hands on the shoulders of the two guys who would choose up sides, one of them was me.

I was so stunned that I didn't react in surprise. I didn't really react at all. I'm sure I looked as if being chosen as a captain happened to me every day. I nodded with a strange out-of-body assurance at Gene, one of the best athletes in the school, who was the other captain.

"Odds or evens?" Coach Fasulo asked, holding his right hand behind his back.

"Odds," I said, which surprised everyone who knew me. It wasn't just that I'd spoken first with such absolute confidence, but that I'd limited myself to a single syllable.

Coach Fasulo held out the formerly hidden hand. His index finger pointed at me. I'd won first choice.

I looked around the gym, tempted to pick the smallest first and strike a blow for every underdog. But I wasn't *that* stupid.

"Red," I said. And even though I was the one doing the picking, it earned me a smile from Red that every kid just can't help showing when he's first chosen.

"Okay!" Red said, stepping to my side of the line.

Gene shook his head. I'd taken his first choice. But he countered with Larry, who could throw a basketball through the hoop from mid-court.

My second pick was Verne, the one kid in the gym smaller than I was. Red stared as me as Verne bounced to join us.

"How come?" Red whispered.

"Little kids are harder to hit," I said. I'd never thought of that before.

"Cool," Red said. "But let's take Frapper next if Gene doesn't grab him." All of a sudden Red and I were co-strategists.

I nodded sagely. "Right." And we got Frapper.

Big, small, athletic, inept, my picks went back and forth. Red seconded every one of them. In no time at all, we had our sides. Coach Fasulo stood at mid-court and then . . .

"GO!"

There's a phenomenon in sports called being "in the zone," like when a quarterback throws for 400 yards and five touchdowns in one game or a golfer birdies on every hole. For the first time in my life, I experienced that feeling. When the three spheres floated into the air, I didn't sprint to the back of the gym. I raced forward with Red by my side and ended up with two of them in my arms while Red held the third.

Everyone on the other team was back-pedaling! I flipped one of the balls to Frapper, who'd come up to complete our triumvirate.

"On three?" Red whispered to me.

"One," I yelled, "two, three!" And then we threw as one.

WHOMP!

BAP!

THUD!

Three outs!

It was a great start for me—and a lucky one. I knew that and contented myself for a while retrieving the balls that bounced off the back wall, feeding them to our front line.

Balls whomped and careened off heads and legs, and then everything started happening faster. I don't remember it all, just flashes like stills pulled from a film.

Hurdling over a ball that whizzed at my ankles and falling back against the padded wall.

Leaping up to latch onto a lob and putting Phil out.

Doing a perfect forward roll to elude a deadly rain of three Bombardment balls aimed right at me.

I do remember, with absolute clarity, the last few minutes of that game. There was a pause in the action, just a split-second, but it was long enough for me to look around and take it all in. The bleachers were packed with players—far more spectators than there'd been at the start. Word had gotten around that a really HOT game was underway.

Only seven players remained on the floor. The three on my team were Red, Verne (who really *had* proved to be hard to hit), and—most unbelievably—me! I'd never even made the final ten before.

Frapper, whose throw had just been caught, was sitting on the front bleacher. He was yelling something my astonished ears could not believe.

"Jumping Joe! Go, Jumping Joe!"

I looked at each of the remaining combatants. The only Joe still standing was me.

I didn't have time to mull that over. The other side held all three of the balls.

"Move back!" Red shouted. "Spread way out!"

Verne wedged himself sideways into the corner. Red

leaned against the back wall. And I just . . . stood there, only twenty feet back from the line.

Gene aimed and fired at my head.

Its impact would have broken not only my glasses, but probably my nose, too. But half a second before it hit, I hopped to the side, felt a breeze brush my face, and heard Coach Fasulo yell, "You're out!"

Who, *me*?

From the other team, Gene shook his head and stalked for the bleaches. I risked a quick glance. Red had caught the ball.

"Jum-pin' Joe!" Frapper yelled again.

The next two shots from the other side found the corner where Verne had sought sanctuary. He was out, but as he ran to the stands, he raised both hands and got a cheer from the crowd.

"You get 'em, Joe," he said as he passed.

And there we stood—Red and I—the last two on our side. Butch Cassidy and a pint-sized Sundance Kid. The Lone Ranger and a tiny Tonto.

Two seconds later Red's shot was caught, and I was nailed in the gut by two balls hurled so hard that one of them bounced off me, through the door of the gym, and down the hall all the way to the principal's office. We were out.

Red pulled me to my feet.

"Great game," he said. The bell that was ringing wasn't just in my head. Everyone was streaming out of the gym.

"Jumpin' Joe, you'll get 'em next time," Frapper said as he passed and punched me hard in the bicep. It was the first time anyone had ever punched me because they *liked* me. Even though it hurt when I flexed that arm, I kept flexing my arm for the rest of the day.

It would be another two years before I'd experience a spurt that would grow me like corn stalk through concrete and help me become a tackle on the football team, a varsity heavyweight wrestler, and a track-team shot-putter. But my growing really started that day, in spirit and self-confidence, if not in body. All because of a game of Bombardment.

Joseph Bruchac

Yes, I was a teenage nerd. I was physically underdeveloped, socially hopeless, and intellectually obnoxious. At the time this photo was taken, the same period during which my story takes place, I was six inches shorter and fifty pounds lighter than I would be by my senior year in high school. In fact, two seconds after my sister snapped this photo, I fell over backwards—overbalanced by the weight of that snowball, which obligingly landed on my face.

For reasons too complicated to explain in a short bio, I was raised by my elderly grandparents in the tiny, rural town of Greenfield Center—three miles from the sophisticated city of Saratoga Springs, where I attended high school. So I was a hick as well as a geek. I loved to read and write, but I loved nature just as much. I was not a couch potato. I spent hours working in the woods with my grandfather and climbing trees and watching birds and animals when I was on my own. Getting involved in sports changed my life for the better, but the time I'd spent in the woods helped me build up the eventual strength and coordination that figured not only into my story of that game of Bombardment, but also my later success in football, wrestling, and track.

My story—my own bio and the tale I've contributed to this anthology—are examples of how we all may grow and change. You never know for sure who you—or the person you might be making fun of—will eventually become.

Two Left Feet, Two Left Hands, and Too Left on the Bench

by

David Lubar

One: Tag—You're Clueless!

Inauspicious. Isn't that a great word? Let it roll off the tongue: in-awe-spish-us. I love words, which—as you'll soon see—is a very good thing. There are all sorts of definitions for this particular word. If you check the dictionary, you'll learn it means "suggesting that the future is unpromising." So, an inauspicious event is a disaster that points toward a whole lot more disasters down the road. Think of it as a bad start.

Better yet, let's define it by example. My first encounter with organized sports was definitely "inauspicious."

I'm not even sure what grade I was in when I decided to join the after-school football program. Second grade sounds about right. I don't remember the gym teacher's name, either. So let's just call him Mr. Growler. The first fact about sports that caught my attention as I wandered toward the field behind the school was that everyone else seemed to have been born knowing not only the rules to the game, but also exactly what to do.

I followed my teammates to one end of the field. "Lubar!" Mr. Growler shouted at me.

"What?" Wow. I'd already been singled out for attention. I decided I loved football.

"You wanna guard?"

Wow again. He was asking me if I wanted to be a guard. Ten seconds into my sporting career, and I was being given an important assignment. Knowing absolutely nothing about the position of a guard in football, and being a total nerd at heart, I figured I should do the one thing I was good at: seek out information. "Where do I stand?" I asked.

"What?" Mr. Growler seemed puzzled.

"Where does a guard stand?" I asked.

He sighed and stared at me as if I'd just arrived from Pluto. Around me, I could hear kids snickering. Mr. Growler pointed at my head. "Would you like a guard for your glasses?"

"Oh . . ." I realized a manly battle like football could be hard on glasses, though, in truth, I had the world's most unbreakable pair. My uncle was an optometrist, and he gave our family free glasses. While that was great for my parents' budget, it meant I ended up with the ugliest, thickest, most unwanted frames on the planet. I could have clubbed an ogre with my glasses. Or hammered together a house. "Yeah, sure, thanks," I mumbled.

And so I started my first game with a padded head guard and no clue whatsoever. Someone on our team kicked the ball. Everyone else ran down the field shouting. I ran down the field shouting.

Everyone stopped running. I wasn't sure why, but I was more than happy to stop, too. We lined up. The other team snapped the ball. (At the time, I had no idea it was called a "snap," but if I limited myself to the sports vocabulary I had back then, this would be a really ugly little passage.) I noticed people all around me were bumping into each other with their arms crossed. A guy from the other team ran toward me. I crossed my arms and ran into him as hard as I could.

He was way bigger than I was. I bounced off to the side. He kept running. But I figured I'd done well. As my moment of sports heroism played through my mind, it occurred to me that this guy was different from the rest of the players. He was clutching a football. Wow—I'd actually bumped the guy who had the ball. Score one for me.

Or so I thought.

After the guy ran the ball into the end zone, my teammates began to question me. "Why didn't you tag him?" "You had him." "What are you doing?" "Don't you know *anything*?"

Did I mention that this was touch football? If I'd had a clue what I was doing, I could have ended the play and been a hero in my very first game merely by uncrossing my arms and touching the guy with the ball.

Instead, I'd been clueless.

Two: What's Round and Bounces and Smells like Fish?

Eventually, I realized that football wasn't my best sport. I discovered I had a passion for basketball. I hung around the playground after school, shooting baskets with anyone who'd let me play. Since it wasn't always easy to convince others to allow me to join their game, what I really wanted was my own basketball. I begged my parents to get me one. I pleaded. But we didn't have a lot of money, and sports equipment was far down the list of things to buy.

Finally, my mom told me she'd seen a special offer from StarKist. If she sent in a bunch of tuna labels and a couple of dollars, she could get me a Charlie the Tuna basketball. (I need to pause here and assure the readers that I am dead serious about this. There honest-to-goodness really was an offer for a Charlie the Tuna basketball. I have no clue what tuna and basketballs have in common, other than the fact that I'd rather not eat either of them raw. And, to tell the truth, as I dredge up these memories, I myself have a hard time believing this. But I swear all of it is true.)

So Mom sent away for it, and eventually my basketball arrived. It was round. It was rubber. It was brownish orange. And it was about two-thirds the size of every other basketball on the planet. Once again clueless, I dribbled it to the playground.

You could hear the laughter six blocks away. In the glorious tradition of guys everywhere, I was severely mocked for having something that wasn't exactly like everyone else's.

Today, small basketballs are cute. They're hot. You can win them at carnivals. Sadly, that wasn't the case back then. I guess I can't blame Charlie the Tuna for keeping me out of the NBA. I'm 5' 8" and can only make a shot when I'm not jumping. But still, every time I see a can of tuna, I shudder just a little.

Three: That Sinking Feeling

As elementary school progressed, I pretty much accepted the fact that I was bad at sports and would always be picked last. But even the least likely kid on a team can have a moment of greatness.

It was a rainy day. We were inside for gym class, playing kickball. When my turn came, I gave the ball a good, hard kick. Which didn't mean anything. My hard kicks could end up dribbling a couple of feet with the wobble of a wounded woodchuck, or flying far foul at frightening angles, or occasionally actually going somewhere useful before being scooped up by an infielder and hurled back at me with terrifying force as I huffed toward first base.

But this one went somewhere. Oh, boy, did it go somewhere. It sailed straight over second base. But that wasn't the end of its glorious trip. It arced all the way across the gym—and then dropped through the basketball hoop on the other side. *Swish.* Nothing but net.

"Automatic home run," Mr. Growler said.

I had no clue about this rule, either. But I rounded the bases, which was something I had never done before (and would never do again).

"That's the first time anyone did that," Mr. Growler told me.

Wow. I'd done something nobody else had ever done. And, finally, after countless humiliating experiences, I'd had my one small moment of glory in the totally meaningless but unbelievably important world of elementary school sports.

Postscript One: Just for Kicks

If this were a work of fiction, that would be the end of the story. But in real life, the moment of glory rarely comes at the right time. After the basket, things returned to normal. In other words, I was hopelessly bad at sports and was often ridiculed. But I survived. Middle school brought moments so awful that I'm not going to even try to put them on paper.

In high school, I went out for fencing. The team was new, and none of us had a clue what we were doing, so I was in good company. It was fun. When the season ended, I wanted to keep in shape, so I signed up for a karate class. Much to my surprise—years after my first disastrous encounter with touch football—I found my sport. Let me say that again. I found my sport. I was actually good at karate. I eventually earned a black belt and even taught classes to others.

It turned out that I'd learned more than I realized. One day, when I was in college, I was with some friends at a local softball field. Someone had brought a bat and ball. Just for fun, I tossed the ball in the air and took a swing.

The ball went right over the fence.

After I bent down and picked up my jaw from where it had dropped on the ground, I realized what had happened. All of the karate practice had helped teach me to focus my power. We had a fun time while I hit flies into the outfield for everyone to catch. Imagine that. Me—hitting balls far into the outfield. If someone had told me back in elementary school that I could put one over the fence with ease, I would have laughed.

Postscript Two: I'll Never Learn

So I grew up, discovered I was a lot better with words than with bats, became a writer, and became a father. Hoping to give my daughter a better start than I had, I signed her up for T-ball when she was in first grade. She seemed to have inherited my skills. After T-ball, she played softball for a couple of years, but didn't like it. I signed her up for basketball. She didn't like that, either.

Finally, one day during the summer before seventh grade, she asked if she could take karate lessons. She was so determined that she actually starting looking through ads in the paper to find a school. To my delight, the school she picked taught a style similar to the one I'd learned. I signed her up. And she was good at it. Really good. She'd found her sport. She won tournaments. She dazzled everyone. She made me proud.

So, what does all of this mean? I guess it means you can survive being a clueless player surrounded by kids who know the rules, and you can survive showing up with a Charlie the Tuna basketball. Really, my friends, you can survive anything. And sometimes, magically, when all you're hoping for is to make it to first base, the ball flies across the gym and swishes through the basket. And sometimes, after looking hard and nearly giving up, you find your sport.

David Lubar

I grew up in Morristown, New Jersey, just a short walk away from Alexander Hamilton Elementary School, where my story takes place. (I'd say it was just a stone's throw, but I never could throw a stone very far.) My home was also right across the street from Morristown High School, where I had many more bad sporting experiences that I'd rather not think about right now. Despite this, one of my books, *Dog Days,* has lots of sports action (along with lots of dog action). My other books include *Hidden Talents* and *Dunk.* My favorite sport is fishing, my favorite football team is the one named after a poem (I hope you can figure out which team that is), and my favorite spectator-sporting event is the Summer Olympics, best viewed from the comfort of my couch. While I still get picked last for anything involving a team, most people who know me will say I'm a good sport about it.

First Position

by

Marilyn Singer

My hands hurt, my legs hurt, but my pride hurt worst of all. I looked sheepishly at Miss Adolph and shrugged. She shook her head and frowned. I heard a few of my classmates tittering. I was never going to climb the ropes in gym class.

I was also never going to hit a home run, sink a basket, beat anyone in a race, or spike a volleyball. I couldn't even serve the ball so it would go over the net. I was the kid who got picked last for every team—if I got picked at all.

I told myself it didn't matter. I had smarts; I had creativity. So what if I wasn't an athlete?

My best friend Karin wasn't an athlete either. She sang in the chorus—solos sometimes. She got the leads in school plays. Everyone thought her voice was fabulous. Nobody cared if *she* couldn't climb the ropes, so she didn't care either.

"Of course we can't do that stuff—we're not monkeys!" she'd always say. "Or guys. Guys have all that upper body strength." She'd make like a strong man and laugh.

I'd laugh, too, but I knew that didn't explain girls like Donna, Alana, or Wendy who could shinny up the ropes almost as fast as any guy—or gibbon.

As soon as the bell rang, I scurried to the locker room, wishing that Karin were there so we could laugh together now. But she had gym at the end of the day, instead of right after lunch when I did. Volleyball or trampoline after tuna sandwiches is not a good idea. Last year I'd thought about making myself barf to get out of class. This year I didn't have to think about making myself do it—it was likely to happen on its own any day now.

Barge was already at her locker next to mine. Her real name was Barbara Gennaro, and she was the biggest girl in fifth grade. Not fat, just very tall and very . . . large. She already had boobs and underarm hair. She climbed the ropes when she felt like it. Everyone was scared of her. We heard she'd wrestled a sixth-grade boy and won!

As I brushed past her, I said, "*Scusa me,*" in a thick, fake Italian accent. I did that every time we had gym. I thought if she thought I was from another country, maybe she'd leave me alone.

She did, giving me nothing more than her usual snort. While I changed my clothes, I tried to hide behind my locker door as much as possible so I wouldn't have to show my twiggy arms and flat chest. Too bad the door was way too short.

"You trying to fit in there?" asked Wendy as she pushed past. Alana was with her. They usually didn't show up until after I was totally dressed—they were too busy sucking up to Miss Adolph by helping put away equipment.

I turned red, but didn't answer. Out of the corner of my

eye, I saw Barge eyeing me either with pity, disgust, or both. "Loser," she had to be saying.

"*Scusa me,*" I repeated, pulled on my shirt, and rushed out of the locker room as fast as my skinny legs would go.

Karin was waiting for me when the final bell rang. She had on her "twinkle face." It meant she knew something I didn't, and she was going to make me guess what it was.

"Guess what we're going to do today."

"Go to your house and eat potato chips?" I replied.

"Nope."

"Buy sparkly knee socks at Schuman's?"

"Nope. Guess again."

"Borrow your brother's BB gun to shoot Wendy and Alana?"

"Huh?"

"*Scusa me.*"

"What?"

"Nothing. I give up. What are we going to do today?"

Karin's face got even twinklier. "We're going to sign up for ballet class."

"Very funny," I said, without laughing.

"I'm not kidding. That new studio finally opened. Alana told me."

"Well, that settles it for sure—if Alana's taking the class, I'm not."

"She's not taking it. Her little sister is. We'll be in a different class."

"We're in a different class, all right," I muttered.

"So, come on. Let's go."

"You're serious? Can you really see me in ballet?"

"Yes," Karin answered—and she wasn't joking. "You can't do softball or volleyball, but you can dance. I've seen you."

"Yeah, but that's only when we're goofing around in my room."

"So? You've got a good imagination. Just imagine the ballet studio is your room!"

"Ha ha. Forget it." But when Karin made up her mind, she made up mine, too.

Karin's mom was happy to agree because it would give her more time to watch soaps and game shows on TV. Mine wasn't so sure.

"You really want to take *ballet*?" Mom said.

I could've stopped the whole thing then and there—a graceful way of telling Karin no way would my folks pay for lessons. But the truth was my favorite paper doll was the one in the Sugar Plum Fairy costume, and I had sometimes fantasized about turning pirouettes on toe shoes. So instead, I got huffy, "Yes! Why not? You think I'm too much of a *klutz*?"

When she hesitated, I wailed, "*MA*!"

"Fine. Take ballet if you want to take ballet," she said, retreating to the coffee pot on the stove, her refuge from pretty much everything.

So Mom and I went shopping together for a leotard and slippers. I wanted a little pink skirt to go with it, but she said if I stuck with it for more than three months, then maybe.

That got me whining again—"Whaddya mean *if I stick with it???*"

"You know very well what I mean," she said, and I did, though I pretended I didn't.

When next Tuesday rolled around and it was time for my first ballet class, I got nervous and tried to wimp out. I told Karin my throat was feeling kind of scratchy, maybe I was coming down with a cold or the flu, and shouldn't I go to bed?

"Stick out your tongue," Karin said briskly.

I did.

"Healthy as a horse," she said, though neither of us had the slightest idea what a healthy horse tongue looked like. "Let's go."

The teacher, Madame Monet, was dressed entirely in black—leotard, tights, long skirt, slippers, and turban. She looked a little like my grandmother, but even thinner. I decided that skinny might be a good thing after all—at least in ballet—until I noticed that her calves and arms had more muscles than I had in my whole body.

"*Bonjour, mes jeunes filles,*" she greeted us.

"*Bonjour, Madame,*" said two of the girls who'd obviously taken ballet before, somewhere.

"*Répétez, s'il vous plaît: 'Bonjour, Madame!'*"

I repeated it along with the rest of the class, wondering if we'd have to learn French to do ballet. Fortunately, Madame Monet switched to English. She explained we'd start with stretching and then learn some of the positions.

The stretching went on forever, but at least it was something I could do. I was actually pretty flexible, though I'd never scored points for that in gym. By the time we got to first position, the class was half over. For the last five minutes, she said we'd do something imaginative: We had to sit on the floor and be mermaids. I closed my eyes, plastered my legs together, and tried to picture myself with a swishing tail. For once, my good imagination failed me. Out of the corner of my eye, I saw Karin prettily swishing her legs back and forth. Well, she was the actress; I wasn't.

"That was fun, wasn't it?" she exclaimed as we were walking home afterwards.

"It was okay," I said.

By lesson five (we had two a week), it was "Okay Minus," sliding toward "No Good." We were still doing a lot of stretching. I didn't mind my occasionally achy muscles because now I could touch my head to my knees, which had earned me a "*Très bien!*" from Madame Monet. We'd gotten to—woo hoo!—second position and also pliés (which were basically sideways knee bends). And we sometimes got to be kelp as well as mermaids (which seemed a step backwards, if you ask me). But pirouettes were a *long* way off. Too long. My pink skirt was a goner—I was beginning to wonder if I'd stick it out for one month, let alone three.

In gym we'd finished with the ropes and other apparatus and were doing "tumbling." I managed to thump my head pretty good during a "forward roll" (Miss Adolph never called it a somersault) and had gotten excused from the rest of the floor exercises that day, which lowered my status even further, if that was possible.

Barge was excused, too. I didn't know why until she produced from her shorts pocket a sanitary pad and marched out of the gym toward the girls' room.

I was so awed I nearly forgot to say "*scusa me*" as I walked past her in the locker room. Then, as if that wasn't overwhelming enough, she asked, "You got yours, too?"

Me? She was talking to *me?* And about . . . *female* . . . things?

"Uh . . . no, no," I replied, still using the fake accent.

That was all I could manage, so Barge just shrugged.

I thought about this brief conversation the whole rest of the day. I even told Karin after school. Karin seemed distracted, though.

"What's the matter with you?" I asked. Then I noticed she didn't have her little pink ballet bag.

"Um . . . I'm really sorry . . . ," she began. I knew what she was going to say.

"You're quitting ballet, aren't you?"

"Um . . . well . . . yeah."

"*Why?*" I said too loudly.

"Well, there's a tap dance class at the same time at my Dad's athletic club, and for musicals it's better if—"

"I can't believe you! You're the one who insisted we take ballet!"

"I know, but . . ."

"But what?"

"But it's . . . boring!" Karin admitted.

I had the perfect out. *Yeah,* I could've said. *It's* really *boring. Let's quit together.*

Instead, whether to prove to myself and my mom that I did have "stick-to-it-ive-ness," or whether I was just feeling contrary, I said, "Well, *I'm* not quitting," and I flounced off to lesson six.

Stretching on the floor, stretching at the barre, first position, second position, plié, and corrections, always corrections. The class had started with twelve students. It was down to seven, and two of them had already studied some ballet. I was thinking what an idiot I was for not having quit, too, when Madame Monet said, "Today we're going to have a little *amusement.*" She said the last word with her French accent. I wondered if there was ever a Barge in her life, too. "Marilyn, come!"

It took a moment before I realized she was calling me. I wasn't bad at ballet, that was true, but no way was I the best.

I was, however, the smallest—and that's why she picked me. "One of the most lovely movements in ballet is the *portée.* Now, Marilyn, I'm going lift you in the air and travel across the floor with you. When I pick you up, open your legs. When I lower you, close them and lightly touch the ground. Can you do that?"

"I don't know," I said, honestly.

She laughed. "Yes, you can." She walked me to one corner of the room. "Now here we go." She lifted me easily and began to glide across the floor. "Open, close, touch. Open, close, touch!" she commanded. I did, and it was amazing. It felt like . . . flying!

"*Encore!*" Madame Monet said when we reached the opposite corner, so back we went. We did two round trips. When she put me down at last, we smiled at each other, and in that instant, I understood why some people lived through the boredom and the aching muscles and broken toes to dance ballet. I was never going to be one of those, but just then it didn't matter. I'd been given the gift of a moment I'd never forget, even after I'd grown up and the ballet school had been turned into a swimming-pool supply store.

I didn't tell Karin about the class. For some reason I wanted to keep it to myself, to hold onto a piece of magic I somehow knew wouldn't happen again. I didn't stay mad at her either. We were too good friends for that.

In gym Miss Adolph told us the next unit would be volleyball, one of my worst sports. I sighed. Wendy and Alana heard me and giggled. Barge must've heard me, too.

Back in the locker room, before I could get out a word, she said, "*Scusa me!*" Instead of shrinking behind my locker door, I started to laugh. She laughed, too. Then she said, "Adolph's not so hot. I could show you how to serve the ball—if you want," she said.

"Yeah?"

"Yeah."

"I could show *you* first position," I said boldly, with no trace of an Italian accent.

"I already know it," Barge replied.

She did, too. And that was something I couldn't *wait* to tell Karin.

Marilyn Singer

I have never been much of an athlete, although I have always liked to dance. I studied tap as an adult for a number of years and ballroom dancing briefly in college. I was pretty good, too.

My experience with ballet was short, but sweet. To this day I remember that feeling of flying through the air. These days, the flying is done by my standard poodle, Oggi. He and I do canine agility—an obstacle course for dogs. He gets to leap over jumps, run through tunnels, run over a seesaw, etc. As for me, I just give him directions and try to stay upright!

For exercise, I walk and stretch a lot in Brooklyn, New York, and Washington, Connecticut, the two places I live with my husband, Steve, and our various pets—and I'd better, after sitting for hours reading and writing. I read and write a lot. So far I've published more than seventy books for children and young adults, including four anthologies which I've edited and to which I've contributed stories.

To learn more about me, please visit my Web site at www.marilynsinger.net.

Finishing Blocks
and Deadly Hook Shots

by

Terry Trueman

I'm in the starting blocks, ready to run the race of my life. As the second-fastest kid at Hillwood Elementary School, I know I have it in me to win this thing. Truthfully, I've never actually lined up against every other kid at Hillwood and raced before, but I know that my best friend Brad can run a little bit faster than me, and I don't know anyone else who can, so I figure I'm second-fastest. But Brad isn't in this race, and even if he were, I think maybe today I could beat him.

It's the Junior Olympics, and kids from schools all over town are here. Seven of us are in this heat. After I win, then I'll go to the semi-finals, and when I win there, I'll go to the finals, and then—you got it—once I win there, I'll officially be the fastest kid in town.

I've never run a race using starting blocks before. It's not a biggie. I mean, they're just these blocks of wood attached to these metal frames, and you're supposed to put your feet against them when you get all bent over at the start. I can just watch what the other kids do, and I'll do the same thing.

I have to keep myself from laughing at all the other guys in the race. They all are wearing actual track shoes with stupid little spikes sticking out the bottom—like *that's* gonna help them. I'm wearing my regular, good-old sneakers, tennis shoes, athletic shoes—whatever you wanna call them—they're good enough for me! I feel really strong and confident!

We're being called to the line now to start the race. I walk over and get in my lane, #3. I'm glad I have this lane so all these other guys can see me pull away from them once I kick it into high gear. This race is only 100 yards long, but that'll give me plenty of time to show everybody what I've got.

The starter is an old guy with a starting gun. He stands to the side like he's kind of bored. I have to admit that there's been about a thousand of these preliminary heats, but he hasn't seen speed like mine yet. He'll probably want my autograph once he sees what I do in this race.

"Take your marks . . . . get set . . ." *BANG!!!*

I fly outta the starting blocks like a cheetah on fire, like the Road Runner escaping Wily Coyote, like a rocket's red glare and bombs bursting in . . . wait a second . . . I'm completely stunned, shocked, amazed to see something I never in a million years thought I might see today—the backs of my opponents as they pull away from me. I bear down and push myself hard, harder, as hard as I can. They're pulling farther and farther away. I glance back over my shoulder and see that one kid is about half a step behind me, way out in lane #6. I'm in second-to-last place!!!!

The six guys who are flying away from me make Brad look like he'd look if he were running this race with a 600-pound gorilla on his back. Some of them actually appear to be shrinking as the distance between us grows greater. And now the kid in lane #6 has caught up with me and is starting to pull away, too.

I push myself as hard as I can, but my legs have turned to spaghetti and my feet feel like they're trapped in giant concrete blocks. This is the most embarrassing moment of my life, and, believe me, I've had my share of embarrassing moments. Suddenly a brilliant idea enters my head: Maybe I'm injured. Maybe I can't run faster today because I have some terrible injury, like to my ankle/leg/hambone/sacroiliac . . . something—*anything* to get me out of this.

I stop running and watch the rest of the racers disappear into the distance. I begin to walk with a fake limp, unable to decide which leg is supposedly hurt, left or right?

Starting blocks, huh? Nope, for me they're finishing blocks, the end of my track-and-field career.

Now basketball is another matter. Hoops, baby! Oh yeah, that's what I'm talking about.

Our pick-up games at lunch and recess here at Hillwood are always an amazing blend of street basketball, full-contact karate, and rugby. I'm almost always one of the first two or three guys picked—Brad and Steve Swinton are the only two guys who are better than me. Actually, a lot of guys never even get to touch the ball because we usually have about fifteen guys per side for our half-court games, so there may be some other good players. But I'm guessing I'm third-best.

Today's contest has been typically brutal. I can't even say how many guys are standing on the sidelines holding ice packs on their heads, and we've only been at it for maybe five minutes.

In yesterday's game I hit a long hook shot—the kind of shot that is unstoppable unless you're like seven feet tall and can jump really high. I mean *long*, too. I must have been twenty feet away from the basket, and I was being guarded by about five guys, and I got myself into position and launched the shot and . . . swish . . . nothing but net. Well, okay, first it hit the backboard, then bounced around the rim a few times, but the important thing is that it went through.

Now I'm only about ten feet out and I'm being guarded by only three other kids. I stop my dribble and eye the basket. Of course, I'm on Brad's team. Steve Swinton sees what's about the happen, and he yells really loudly, **"WATCH TRUEMAN! HE'S DEADLY ON THOSE HOOKS!!!"**

He's got that right. Deadly!

At the sound of Steve's panicked yell, everybody in the gym freezes and looks straight at me. I take my single step away from the basket, lift my arm in a perfect, gorgeous sweeping motion . . . this shot feels just right. Watch me, everyone, I'm deadly on these hooks!!! Hoops, baby, . . . my game . . . oh yeah . . . deadly!!!!!

What happened? What's wrong? Well, the obvious answer is that the ball missed by a little . . . uh, no, that's not actually true . . . the 'little' part. The ball went a good fifteen feet over the top of the backboard—I think it actually scraped the ceiling of the gym. I didn't even know I could throw a ball that high. It looks like the ball got launched from one of those old-fashioned catapult things that threw big fireballs over the tops of palace walls back when guys used to wear armor and stuff.

There is no armor thick enough to save me from the laughter that echoes through the gym now. Steve Swinton is speechless and is probably the only kid in the room who could be even one-hundredth as embarrassed as I am. "Watch Trueman! He's deadly on those hooks," is no doubt the way he wishes he'd said it—but not nearly as much as he wishes he hadn't said it at all.

It's ten minutes later, and I'm standing on the side of the gym floor doing the only thing I could think to do: holding an icepack on my "hurt" wrist.

When the game is finally over, Brad walks up to me and asks, "You all right?"

I answer, "Oh yeah, I'll be okay . . . just a little . . . I don't know . . . tendonitis of the wrist joint in the carpal tunnel vein or something."

"Uh huh," Brad says, then he looks at me a little bit closer and says, "It's funny that it's your left wrist that's hurt. The way you threw that hook shot up, I thought it must be your shooting hand."

I look down at my icepack and quickly move it to my other wrist. "Yeah, sorry," I say.

Brad just smiles at me.

Finishing blocks and deadly hook shots—

Thank goodness, there's always baseball!!

Terry Trueman

Growing up in Seattle, every kid in my neighborhood suspected that he might have the right stuff to "go pro" in the sport of his choice when he reached adulthood. Okay, maybe not *every* kid—but I definitely did! When I was a kid, my best pal was a guy my age named Brad Sather who was actually, in fact, *better* than I was at every sport we tried. I honestly thought that next to Brad, I was the best. Life can be shockingly filled with disappointing reality, you know? Well, at least Plan B—the writing thing—has worked out pretty well.

Finding High-Jump Fame: A Shorts Story

by

Dorian Cirrone

I took a bite of my salami sandwich and stared at the engraved wooden plaque across from me: *Sabal Palm Elementary School Track Records.* Because we didn't have a gym, the cafeteria was the place where sports and sloppy joes were forced to meet. Something I would not recommend in real life.

I ran my eyes down the plaque and stopped at my name. Well, it wasn't exactly my name. It was half my name. The other half belonged to my younger brother, Chris.

Chris Cirrone, fifth-grade superstar, girl magnet, and now, Sabal Palm Elementary School Boys High Jump Record Holder. Don't get me wrong. I was proud of my brother. I loved my brother. But it wasn't that easy being a year older and known around school as "Chris's sister." If I had a pair of shorts for every time I was called that, I could have clothed the world.

Kids I didn't even know would come up to me and ask, "Is it true you're Chris's sister?"

I'd nod while they'd stare me up and down and then walk away. It happened enough times that I knew not to expect any praise for my own accomplishments.

It wasn't always that way, though. I'd had my taste of celebrity in third grade when I was the Sugar Plum Fairy in the class production of *The Nutcracker*. For a brief, shining moment, after we performed for the whole school, everyone knew who I was. I even had a couple of second-grade groupies.

But somehow my fairy fame was fleeting. By fourth grade, it was back to being a nobody.

The whole high jump thing might have been easier to take if I'd known that my brother had practiced day and night to become a superstar. But, no, it wasn't like that. A few weeks before, at the beginning of track season, he had been asked to stand in for another high jumper who'd gotten sick. My brother had already won a couple of ribbons that day for running the 50-yard dash and a relay race by the time Mr. C asked him to take the place of the absent jumper.

The way my brother told it, he hadn't really worked on the high jump much. It wasn't his specialty. He'd watched some athletes on television and saw how they cleared the bar doing a jump called the "Western Roll" instead of the traditional "Scissor Jump," in which you kicked one leg up and then the other.

"The Western Roll." Who would have thought something that sounded like an egg-and-ham sandwich could bring you fifth-grade fame?

It turned out that my brother's new move was kind of like a swimming dive. Instead of the legs going over the bar first, the hands did. Then the rest of the body followed, stomach down, twisting slightly to the side.

The first time my brother "rolled" over the bar successfully at about four feet, "oohs" and "aahs" rippled throughout the crowd. No one had ever seen a move like that at our elementary school track meets. The coaches held a brief meeting to see if it was even allowed.

Once it was determined that my brother wasn't breaking any of the Supreme Court of High Jumping laws, he was allowed to go forth with his Western Roll.

The bar was set at 4'1". He cleared it easily.

Then 4'2". Again, no problem.

Soon, it was just Chris and the bar. He'd already cleared 4'4", easily winning the blue ribbon. But he had to clear one more inch before setting a new school record. The crowd was silent as he soared over the bamboo pole.

Thunk! My brother landed in the sawdust with the bar still intact. The crowd cheered wildly.

"You want to try for four-six?" Mr. C asked.

My brother nodded and ran back to the starting spot.

He ran. He rolled. He aced it. And the crowd cheered again.

At 4'7", my brother's toe clipped the bar, and it landed in the sawdust next to him. The crowd sighed. But it didn't matter. The old Sabal Palm Elementary School High Jump record had been broken. The new one was now 4'6", a full two inches higher than the last.

I recalled my brother's day of glory and stared at the numbers on the plaque. My eyes trailed over to the girls' side. The high-jump record stood at 3'8".

I'd cleared 3'6" at practice, making me eligible for the next big track meet, the last one of the season. I wondered if I had a shot at breaking the record. I was a sixth grader, ready to go to junior high the next year. If I didn't break it now, I'd never get another chance at elementary school fame.

My dance classes had given me an edge over a lot of jumpers. All those high kicks, which we called *grand battements* in ballet class, made it easier for me to master the Scissor Jump.

For the next week, I practiced every day after school. I wasn't brave enough to try the Western Roll. But I worked like a Rockette on my high kicks, hoping they'd be my ticket to becoming a sports celebrity like my brother.

Each day I'd stand back, stare at the bar, and picture myself soaring over it with ease. And each day, I'd hit 3'7" and nick the bar with some part of my body. I was stuck at 3'6".

On the morning of the last track meet, I put my yellow shorts on under my skirt and hoped they'd bring me good luck. The shorts weren't a fashion statement. They were a sports necessity. Back then, girls had to wear skirts or dresses to school. And there were no gym suits until seventh grade. We all got into the habit of wearing shorts every day, and we took off our skirts for physical education class.

I could hardly concentrate all day as my teachers explained the importance of knowing about fractions and sentence fragments. The only fraction I was interested in was that fraction of an inch that would hand me the girls' high-jump record.

When three o'clock arrived, I raced out to the field. Sabal Palm was hosting the meet, so the kids who'd come from other schools were already warming up.

"Hey, there you are!" a voice from behind me shouted. It was my friend Kathy, who lived next door. She'd come to watch the meet. I was relieved to see a friendly face.

I handed her my notebook. "Will you hold this a minute while I take off my skirt?"

"Sure," Kathy said. "Want me to keep your stuff while you're jumping?"

"Yeah, thanks," I said. "I've got to go warm up. See you in a while."

Kathy tucked my skirt under her arm. "Good luck!" she yelled.

I raced toward the other high jumpers and began practicing my kicks. I stretched out my calf muscles and gazed around at my competition. *Not too bad*, I thought.

When it was time for the event, everyone crowded around the huge letter *H* made by the high-jump poles.

We started at 3'2". All ten girls cleared the bar. When it was raised to 3'3", one girl tripped and ruined her jump. When it was my turn, I heard a tiny ripping sound as my feet left the ground. I was nervous for a second, but when I landed in the sawdust with the bar still intact, my worries disappeared.

Nine of us were left, and the bar was raised to 3'4". The girl before me dropped out. This time, as I kicked my right foot up, I heard an even louder rip. After I cleared the bar, I glanced down at my shorts and found a two-inch slit in the inside seam.

I ran to get back in line, a little worried about the new air-conditioning in my shorts. Sweat trickled down my forehead as I moved up for another turn.

When the bar was raised to 3'5", my muscles began to twitch with excitement and nervousness. I took a deep breath before my turn.

I ran. I jumped. I ripped. I aced it. But the tear was even bigger now. It reached from the hem of one inside seam all the way up to the crotch of my shorts. So far, no one seemed to notice.

When they raised the bar to 3'6", seven of us were left. I stared at the horizontal pole, thinking more about my splitting seam than sports stardom. I wondered if it would be better to stop now rather than risk the embarrassment of exposing myself to the entire track meet. But if I dropped out, Mr. C would want to know why. I prayed that my shorts would hold out for another jump.

Again, I held my breath. I ran and jumped. And this time, I really ripped. As I cleared the bar, the whole seam gave way and my shorts became a skirt, flapping in the breeze. I heard the crowd gasp.

I looked up at the bar and almost wished it had fallen. What could I do? I couldn't jump again with my shorts like that.

Then, out of nowhere, I felt a hand in mine. It was Kathy, and she was pulling me away from the track meet and toward the portable classrooms at the edge of the field. We ran between two portables. She looked around like a spy and slipped her shorts out from under her skirt.

"Here," she said, "put these on."

My heart pounded as I unzipped my own shorts and for a brief moment stood in my underwear. I pulled on Kathy's shorts without saying a word.

I looked down. They were short and puffy and had blue flowers on them. My lucky yellow shorts weren't going to do me any good now.

"What are you doing?" Kathy said. "Run. Get back there."

I did what she said and slipped back in line just in time for my turn. There must have been snickering, but I didn't hear a thing as I focused on the shape of the bars.

Maybe it was me. Maybe it was the shorts. Or maybe I just wanted to get as far away from that field as possible. But at 3'7" I knocked the bar right into the sawdust with me. Now I understood. The big *H* stood for "Ha!"

I didn't wait to see who won. I ran to Kathy and got my stuff. I left her at the meet to watch more events and walked home.

The next morning when I met Kathy to walk to school together, I gave her the shorts back. "Thanks," I said.

"Sorry they didn't bring you good luck."

I laughed. "They were better than mine," I said. "At least yours didn't expose my underwear to the entire track meet."

Kathy laughed. "I guess they did their job then."

Up until gym class, no one said anything about the track meet. A lot of the kids who had seen what happened were from other schools. By the time gym class came, I thought I was home free. But as we lined up for roll call, Mr. C said he had an announcement.

"We had an incident at the track meet yesterday," he said. His voice sounded serious, but his face revealed a hint of amusement.

I quickly gazed out at the empty track field to avoid his eyes.

"And I want to remind you all, especially the girls, to make sure that you don't wear shorts that are too tight."

A couple of kids immediately turned my way. Then,

little by little, everyone's eyes were on me. My face burned as a wave of snickers and whispers washed over the class. As Mr. C shushed them, the truth became painfully obvious. Not only had I *not* reached high-jump fame, but I had landed right into a pile of high-jump shame.

There were no more track meets after that one. And when I started junior high the next year, I wasn't so eager for high-jump fame. I joined the newspaper staff instead—something that didn't require wearing shorts.

But I learned two things from that experience:

I learned that Kathy was a really good friend. And sometimes having a really good friend can be just as good as having a whole bunch of people you don't know think you're really cool.

I also learned that you sometimes find fame in the strangest places. About ten years after my brother broke the high-jump record, someone else broke it, and my brother's name was removed from the plaque. But I'm pretty sure for a long time after that, Mr. C was still telling the story about the girl whose shorts split during the high jump as a warning to the kids in his gym classes not to wear their shorts too tight.

It wasn't what I had in mind. But fame is fame, and you might as well take it—wherever it comes from.

Dorian Cirrone

Once I realized I was not going to find fame doing the high jump, I started searching for it in other places. In high school, I began taking my dance classes more seriously and eventually became a teacher and choreographer. While in college, I taught ballet, tap, and jazz for several years. But I did not find fame as a dancer.

After that I started working for a local newspaper as a typist and eventually worked my way up to feature writer and then assistant city editor. But I did not find fame as a journalist.

After several years at the newspaper, I went to graduate school to study English and taught freshman composition classes. No fame there either.

While raising my two children, I returned to something I'd always loved: writing. After many years of working on the craft, I began publishing some poetry, a memoir, and literary criticism in journals and anthologies and then, finally, a young adult novel, *Dancing in Red Shoes Will Kill You.* A chapter book tentatively titled *Lindy Blues* will be published next year. I hope to continue looking for fame in the publishing world.

Some days, though, I wonder if my life would have turned out differently if I'd just worn looser shorts back in sixth grade.

Line Drive

by

Tanya West

Growing up the oldest sister of three brothers doesn't always make you a tomboy, but it helps. And having a mom who would rather punt a football than sew a quilt sets the stage for some great sports memories, too. Obviously, no one ever told me that girls couldn't play baseball or ride a boy's bike or wrestle Indian-style. I could smack a grimy hardball across the fence with the best of the neighborhood boys—and I was just a skinny, short girl with glasses. Mom taught us—her sons and daughters—how to do all those things. A former baton twirler and field hockey maven, my mom was the next best thing to a real coach.

In fact, Mom usually showed up early with my brothers for Little League and helped the head coach "warm up the boys" by hitting line drives, grounders, and high fly balls. My brothers seemed caught between being really proud of Mom and being completely mortified that this five-foot-short lady could hammer a line drive to third while faking out the first baseman. I guess she figured she should do everything she could to be both a mom and dad to us kids. Actually, most dads couldn't hit and throw as well as she could. Or yell as loudly from the bleachers. But that's another story.

I think my first baseball glove must have been a cast-off from my one-year-younger brother, Bobby. It didn't matter. I was following in my mother's cleats. Bobby and I played pass, practiced pitching and catching, and teased our littler brother, Ricky, with games of keep-away. As soon as Ricky started catching more than missing, he joined us, too. That was when real baseball happened. One pitcher, one catcher, one batter. It was the best. We took turns playing each spot until it grew too dark to see the old, brown baseball.

My brothers didn't mind that I was a girl. Actually, I'm not even sure they noticed—until we moved across the street from Mark. Mark ran the dead-end neighborhood we had just joined. He was the loudest, mouthiest eleven-year-old I'd ever seen. His idea of playing catch with his dog was to throw the ball into the biggest bush he could find and then laugh and laugh when Sarge couldn't get past the brambles to retrieve it. Did I mention Mark was an only child? He was not used to sharing—especially the spotlight.

We had lived in our duplex farmhouse only a few weeks before Little League started. In those days, girls weren't allowed to play on the boys' teams. And there weren't any girls' teams. None. Zero. Nada. The only way I could sit on the bench with the guys was as the scorekeeper. So I learned all about lineups and substitutions and "the rules" of playing. The only rule I could never understand was unspoken: "No girls on the team." Mom could warm up the team, but I had to sit on the sidelines holding a pencil instead of a baseball.

Bobby and Ricky were close enough in age—nine and ten—to be on the same team. Tall, lanky Bobby reigned in the outfield or on first base. Short, quick Ricky started out at shortstop, but found his real place squatting behind the batter as the world's smallest catcher. And the pitcher Ricky had to catch for was usually Mark.

To say Mark was conceited about his pitching skills is like saying Godzilla was a big lizard. After striking out a batter, Mark would take off his ball cap, run his fingers through his curly black hair, and flash a wide smile at the giggling girls on the bleachers. Sure, he was cute. Cute as a rabid hamster.

Bobby and Ricky found a way to get along with Mark. They just reminded him how good he was as often as possible. Thing is, he *was* good. No one could pitch as fast or as straight as Mark. He was all-star material, all right. And he made sure everyone knew it. I didn't like the sneer that so often slid across his face from one ear to the other. But I loved to watch him pitch. As I marked down the strikeouts in the team's scorebook, I knew this guy had something special. The coach loved him, the fans loved him, and he loved himself. And—I had to admit it—I was impressed with this jerk and his fastball.

I felt my palms sweat when he'd sometimes have to sit beside me on the bench, waiting for his turn at bat. I squeaked every time I said, "Mark, you're on deck!" And I watched as he stood in the circle, practicing his swing and smiling at the crowd—but never at me. Who was I, anyway? Just the skinny girl with glasses who kept score.

Sometimes my brothers still played baseball with me in our backyard. But if Mark was home, they took off for his yard and left me in the dust. You'd think there was another girl in the neighborhood for me to play with, but there wasn't. If I was going to hang out with anybody, it was going to have to be with Bobby, Ricky, and Mark. And if Mark was ever going to notice me, it would have to be on his terms—playing baseball.

"Let me come with you," I begged one afternoon when my brothers were getting ready for a neighborhood game in Mark's yard. "I can play as well as you can. Just let me come and play outfield."

"I don't know," said Bobby. "Mark wouldn't like it. You're a girl. He doesn't have a sister or anything. You oughta stay home."

"Let me just try," I begged. "If he doesn't want me to play, I'll go home. I promise."

Bobby looked at Ricky, who just shrugged and tossed a short pop-up to catch.

"All right. But if he gets mad, you have to go home. Okay?"

"Okay," I agreed. I was happier than a mouse in a corn-crib. I grabbed my old glove and followed the boys down the long gravel lane toward Mark's house, grinning so big that my cheeks pushed my glasses off my nose.

I stood in Mark's side yard, the designated baseball area, where the bases were brown spots of naked dirt. A plank of wood was half-buried in the middle—the pitcher's mound, Mark's territory. I stood on it for a second, balancing myself and looking straight ahead at the home-plate patch. I heard the guys emerge from the porch, Mark laughing at something Ricky had said. When I looked over, I could tell they hadn't mentioned anything about me coming over to play.

Mark stared at me standing there on his pitcher's plank and stopped.

"What's she doing here?" he asked. "We don't need a scorekeeper."

Bobby lifted his ball cap and scratched his head. "She just wants to play outfield. Is that okay?"

Mark kept staring. Then the smirk started, little at first, then spreading over his face. "I'll tell ya what," he said, looking at me but talking to my brothers. "If she can hit one of my pitches, she can play."

My brothers both looked like they could have caught a fly—in their mouths!

"Uh–uh–uh," Bobby tried to respond.

Ricky just shook his head. After all, no one knew the sting of Mark's pitches better than he did. He'd caught a lot of them as they whipped past the batters and into the catcher's mitt.

"Okay," I said.

My brothers blinked hard, like they hadn't really heard what they'd really heard.

"Okay," I repeated.

Now, don't misunderstand me. I wasn't brave. I wasn't even sure *I'd* heard what I'd said. But I knew I wanted to play—and I wanted to hang out with Mark somehow, some way. This was my chance.

Bobby took first base, Ricky headed behind me to catch, and Mark claimed the throne—the pitcher's mound. I picked up the wooden bat that had Mark's name chiseled in the handle. It was heavy, but I wrapped my hands around it pretty well. My heart started to beat all the way into my ears. As I took a couple of practice swings, I realized that I was all lined up to be a dead girl. In less than a second, I could be hit by a baseball traveling the speed of a car on the interstate. And all the guys would say was: "She said she wanted to play."

Mark turned sideways and started his windup. I could sense Ricky's little body squatting lower as Mark got ready to launch the pitch.

Zing!

Snap!

Right into Ricky's mitt. I never even saw it.

"Strike one!" Mark called. A grin seemed to spread all over his head. I could tell he was thinking that it would take only two more pitches to finish me off.

I pounded the ground with the top of the bat and took another swing.

Just swing as soon as you see him let go, I told myself. This wasn't going to be about skill. This was going to be about luck—good or bad.

Mark caught the ball Ricky tossed back to him. He took his place back on the plank and turned sideways, staring right at me this time. I watched every little move. The settling of his arms down as he held the ball in his right hand and hid it inside the glove on his left. Then the knee, slowly lifting upward until it nearly touched his elbow. He leaned forward as his foot went down, and I watched as his right arm arched over his head, the ball barely peeking out from his fist. Then he let go . . .

And I swung as hard as I could.

Crack! The wood vibrated in my hands, and I dropped the bat.

"O-o-o-f," Mark seemed to be sucking in all the air in the neighborhood. His arms dropped to his sides, and the ball dribbled down his front and fell flat in front of him. I'd hit a line drive—right into Mark's gut.

He curled up on the ground, moaning and gasping for air. My brothers raced over to their star pitcher, but were afraid to get too close.

"You okay, man?" Ricky asked.

Mark moaned. I thought I saw a tear in the corner of his eye. Probably not.

"Hey, I'm really sorry," I said. But I wasn't. I was exhilarated! I was victorious! And I was in big trouble.

"I think you'd better go home," Bobby told me. I don't know if he was mad at me or scared for me.

Mark caught part of his breath just then. "Nah, . . . she doesn't have to," he half-whispered. "A deal's a deal." He looked up at me and I saw a real smile. "At least you don't hit like a girl," he said.

"Sure I do," I answered. "I hit just like my mom."

And nobody could argue with that.

Tanya West

I eventually traded the neighborhood games for lunch-hour intramural games in junior high school and found my best sport was volleyball. By the time I entered high school, girls' teams were just beginning to catch on in my hometown. I earned a varsity letter in volleyball each of my four years and continued to play on coed leagues in college. You haven't lived until you've had a 6'4" guy slam a spike into your head! After college, I taught high school

English and social studies and actually coached girls' sports: volleyball, basketball, and track. It was a time of getting cast-off uniforms and not enough practice time (because the boys needed the gym more), but we ladies were just happy to have a chance to compete.

I've had the fun of raising three sons and playing backyard baseball, games of P-I-G, and putt-putt golf. Sometimes I even let them win! And I think they've learned that sports aren't just for jocks—they're for anyone who gets a kick out of a good game.

Today I work as a writer and editor and wish I had more time for my newest sport: tennis.

Riding the Century

by

Alexandra Siy

At seven, I had radically short hair, wore boy's sneakers, and went topless all summer. My grandmother, the only person who called me Alexandra instead of Alex, was horrified.

"I might as well have *five* grandsons!" she said. "What happened to ballet?"

Grandmother was terrifying in her heavy perfume and giant clip-on earrings. Despite my tough appearance, I was too scared to tell her that I was kicked out of ballet class for contorting my body into pretzel shapes and making faces in the mirror when I thought the teacher wasn't looking. Anyway, wasn't it obvious that I was way too big and ugly for ballet—that I looked a lot better in pack boots than in ballet slippers?

Little League Baseball, not ballet, was what I wanted. But girls weren't allowed to play, so I spent my Saturday afternoons on the bleachers watching my brothers and hoping that the rules would change.

By the time I was ten I could hit farther, throw harder, and run faster than all my brothers, but the rules still hadn't changed. Injustice, I decided, was when you could beat them but you couldn't join them.

It was 1970, and I was old enough to know that I wasn't the only person in the world with a problem. All I had to do was turn on the TV—Vietnam, racial prejudice, the Cold War, pollution—it was all there for me to see.

But I'd also watched men walk on the moon. I believed that things could change and great things could happen.

Although I didn't know it then everything changed the day my mother bought herself a bicycle. Before that, we hadn't paid each other much attention: I was busy collecting baseball cards and memorizing Major League statistics while she was occupied washing diapers, ironing sheets, and making pot roast.

Mommy's new bicycle was cause for concern. Was it right, I wondered, for a mother to buy herself a bicycle, ride around town, and write down her mileage in a notebook? Didn't normal mothers stay at home baking cupcakes—the kind with buttercream frosting and red sprinkles? So, when Mommy asked me to come along one day, I was slightly confused and quite annoyed.

"Riding around town on your brand-new bicycle might be fun for you, but do you really expect me to be seen on the Toilet Seat Bike?" I asked.

The so-called Toilet Seat Bike was my single-speed, lima-bean-green, balloon-tire bike with broken seat springs that cost a dollar at a yard sale. In order to ride it you had to put down the seat, just like before sitting on the toilet. With four brothers I'd had enough of putting down the toilet seat.

"Who's looking at you?" Mommy answered.

That's what she always said about everything. Like the horrid shoes with the buckles, the shrunken knee socks, and the skirt with the orange zigzags that she made me wear for my class photo. (I still have that picture, and even now when I look at it I'm totally embarrassed.)

"Maybe nobody's looking at you, but they're looking at *me,*" I snapped. "I am not riding around in public on a toilet seat."

"Then ride your brother's bike," she said, which sounded more like a command than a suggestion.

One ride led to another, and soon I was pedaling my brother's unwieldy old Schwinn through a sweltering potato field on Long Island. Mommy was just a dot in the distance.

"Wait up!" I yelled.

But she was too far away to hear. When I finally caught up she was waiting in a motel parking lot.

"This place has a pool," she said, "let's get a room."

And what a pool it was—oval shaped, with a twisty slide and a bouncy diving board! I stayed in until my fingers and toes were pale and wrinkled like those nasty baby hot dogs that come in jars. That sensational pool made every miserable mile worthwhile and also convinced me that bike riding with Mommy was actually fun.

What a relief that must have been for her, because who else would she have dragged along? Certainly not my father, who loved spectator sports, especially horse racing.

Shortly after our Long Island junket, Mommy joined a bicycle club called the Mohawk-Hudson Wheelmen. She stayed up late at night drawing maps with titles like "Basic-Bear Swamp Tour" and tapping out articles for *The Bikeabout* newsletter on her IBM Selectric.

And she took me along to all the bike club meetings.

"Now," she said, "you have something else to do besides sitting on the bleachers at the Little League park every Saturday afternoon."

But I couldn't just forget about my fantasy of playing Little League—of one day putting on a real baseball uniform, stepping up to the plate, and hitting a home run out of the park. The spring I was eleven I still hoped that this would be the year they finally changed the rules.

But it wasn't.

Perhaps Mommy felt sorry for me, or maybe she just wanted to make sure I'd keep going along with her on bike rides. Whatever the reason, she bought me a new bike.

It wasn't a cool 10-speed with turned-down handlebars and skinny tires. But it was infinitely superior to the shameful Toilet Seat Bike. Sparkly blue, it had three speeds that shifted with a flick of the thumb. It even had a plastic basket attached to the handlebars and white streamers trailing from its glittery handgrips.

All that Little League season long Mommy and I racked up mileage in the bicycle notebook, and when the summer was over she made an announcement.

"I've signed us up for the Century."

"Aren't we already in the middle of one?" my father asked, a bit sarcastically from his chair in front of the TV.

"A Century is one hundred miles," Mommy answered, "in twelve hours or less."

We started from a church parking lot at 8 o'clock on a Saturday morning. All of my mother's bicycling friends were there—an unusual crowd.

Claire Boink, for example, had what appeared to be a custom-made, extra-wide bicycle seat. Betty Lou Bailey, on the other hand, was pointy and sharp, and looked alarmingly like the Wicked Witch of the West in *The Wizard of Oz.* (At any moment, I wondered, might Toto jump out of that pannier?)

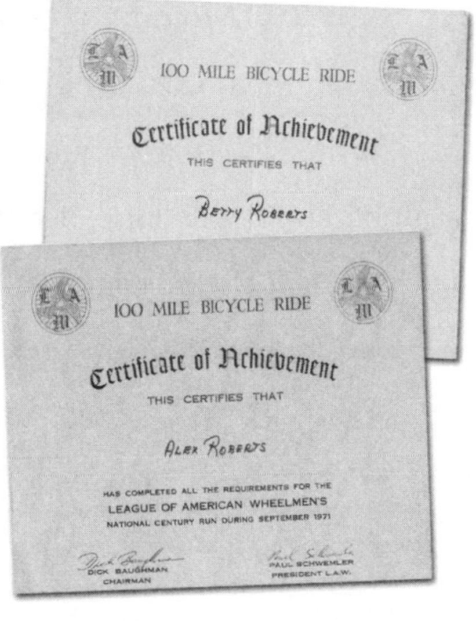
100 MILE BICYCLE RIDE

Certificate of Achievement

THIS CERTIFIES THAT

Betty Roberts

100 MILE BICYCLE RIDE

Certificate of Achievement

THIS CERTIFIES THAT

Alex Roberts

HAS COMPLETED ALL THE REQUIREMENTS FOR THE
LEAGUE OF AMERICAN WHEELMEN'S
NATIONAL CENTURY RUN DURING SEPTEMBER 1971

DICK BAUGHMAN
CHAIRMAN

PAUL SCHWEMLER
PRESIDENT L.A.W.

But even more fascinating than her resemblance to the infamous film star was her bicycle: an ultra-light, 10-speed, gadget-loaded French road bike. With its speedometer, odometer, bells, blaze-orange flag, front and rear generators, plastic fenders, toe clips, and twin mirrors, Betty Lou Bailey's bike matched her personality, exactly.

And then there was the Lance Armstrong of the club, Bob Wilcox, dressed in padded nylon shorts and a Spiderman-tight, banana-colored jersey. His special shoes locked into hooks on his pedals, and he wore a skimpy (to what good?)

helmet. Bob Wilcox, whom Mommy referred to in reverent tones (I think she liked him), never actually spoke to me and probably never saw me through his heavy-framed glasses.

As usual, Mommy and I had on our polyester windbreakers and cutoffs.

"Who's looking at you?" she whispered, when I complained about our lack of cycling fashion. But she sounded far less shrill than usual.

And as always, Mommy wore her hideous pink, pointy-toed Keds, of which I was more embarrassed than anything else in the world. Why, for once, wouldn't she take my lead and get some Converse All Stars? Thank God, I thought, all the other kids in America were at home in their pajamas watching Bugs Bunny and eating Fruit Loops.

We started together, eagerly coasting downhill, but by the time we were on the uphill, everyone except for Claire Boink and an old guy on a giant tricycle was far ahead.

We rode steadily, Mommy in front. I watched the muscles in her legs bulge and pop each time they pushed the pedals. I looked down, trying to see if my own legs were as powerful, and almost rammed into her. When we stopped at the top of a big hill for a drink of water, Mommy spread her arms, as if hugging the sky.

"It reminds me of Grandma Moses," she said.

Had a lack of oxygen impaired her memory?

"I thought your grandmother was dead," I said.

"She's a painter, not my grandmother."

I lost sight of Mommy as we sped downhill into the scenic valley. Squeezing my vibrating handgrips while trying to keep my wheels from wobbling out of control, I almost panicked. Did Mommy turn? I took my eyes off the pavement for a split second to look down an empty crossroad.

As I flew along the flats and regained control of my bike, I took a big breath—I guess I'd been holding it. No mother should be able to ride a bike so fast!

When I finally caught up, Mommy was sitting on a grassy hill next to a bridge.

"Doesn't this look like a nice spot for lunch?" she asked.

I flopped onto the grass and devoured my natural peanut butter on whole grain bread.

"Carrots?" Mommy asked, handing me a soggy wax paper baggie. "Apple?"

"Don't we have anything less crunchy?" I asked.

Unfortunately Mommy had just discovered *Diet for a Small Planet.* Her experiments with recipes, such as sugarless cookies, were bad news for a girl who cherished McDonald's Hot Apple Pies. So when she handed me a Milky Way bar I was more than kind of shocked.

I ate the candy as slowly as possible, savoring its fluffy core as if it were the last Milky Way in the universe. Mommy interrupted my concentration with a rare confession.

"Alex, did you know that I used to fly one of those?" she asked, pointing at the small airplane that buzzed overhead.

"You did?" I answered, more than amazed, once again. "Does Daddy know?

"I took flying lessons when I was eighteen," she said, "before I met him."

The candy bar was gone, and my mind was whirring: What other secrets did she keep? But the time for chitchatting was over. The clock was ticking.

"We took too long a break," Mommy said. "My legs are stiff."

"Mine too," I said, "they feel like concrete."

Mommy had just put on her sunglasses and was studying the roadmap when she suddenly gasped.

"We're lost!"

"What?"

"Look it," she said, "I think we're here, and the route is here . . . I thought we were on this road, but we're on this one . . ."

We'd already gone five miles off-course.

"Well, we'll just have to turn around," she said, matter of fact.

"What?" I repeated. "Turn around and add even more miles?"

"What else can we do?" she said, getting on her bike.

We rode all afternoon like there was someone chasing us. By the time we were on the sixty-sixth mile, I figured I might as well have been riding the Toilet Seat Bike, because having three speeds didn't feel any easier than one.

What did I think about as the sun scorched my forehead and salty sweat dripped from my temples into the corners of my dusty-dry mouth?

An ice-cold orange soda in a glass bottle that costs a dime from the old-fashioned vending machine at Meyer's Riding Ranch on Flat Rock Road . . . jumping into the spring-fed creek behind our house . . . playing hide-and-seek in the basement.

A vanilla ice cream cone dipped in chocolate.

Skiing, by far my favorite of all sports, loved more than even baseball . . . which reminds me of my favorite Major League player, Johnny Bench, and how cute he is and maybe that's really why I like baseball so much . . .

. . . and why won't Mommy stop for a drink?

"Wait up!" I yelled.

My heart raced as I pushed up another hill, trying to catch her. I could see her up ahead, her skinny back bent into the wind that whipped up suddenly, as it often does in the late afternoon on splendid fall days.

I listened to the chain click each time I pedaled.

There's a kind of beat to bike riding, like music, and I went along with it until a car rushed by, a little too close, forcing me into the ditch.

Mommy looked back over her shoulder, her forehead wrinkled with worry. So she *did* have eyes in the back of her head, just like any-old ordinary mother.

"I'm okay," I yelled.

But she soon pulled out of sight again.

"Stop!" I shouted into the emptiness.

Suddenly, a terrible thought crossed my mind. The more I thought about it, the more I was convinced:

I would quit.

"I'm quitting!" I yelled.

Maybe Mommy had bionic ears in addition to her supernatural legs and could hear my threat.

"I'm stopping right now!" I screamed.

Attempting to get within her earshot, I pedaled faster and faster until I was tearing around a curve. The crazy idea of crashing my bike into the hedge that seemed to be rushing toward me popped into and out of my head.

I squeezed down hard on my handbrakes and skidded to a stop, suddenly face-to-face with a cow.

She looked at me with her big, bored, glossy eyes and yawned.

Up ahead I could see Mommy waiting, looking like a leafless tree silhouetted against the darkening sky.

"It's too dark to ride," she said as I pulled alongside her. "We can't go on."

Just a few minutes earlier I was convinced that I was finished. But hearing Mommy say we had to stop was utterly unacceptable.

"You mean we rode all this way for nothing?" I demanded.

"It's just too dangerous riding in the dark," Mommy answered, pushing her bike to the side of the road.

A car approached, its headlights blinding.

"See," she said, squinting, "that guy can't even see us."

We pulled farther into the ditch, but the car slowed down and someone shouted from the window.

"Keep going, we'll follow you!"

"It's Claire Boink!" Mommy shouted.

A parade of headlights lit up the highway as we stood up on our pedals and rode on.

"You're almost there!" called a man.

Then Betty Lou Bailey pedaled up beside us.

"Just keep it going," she panted, jingling her bells.

"Seven minutes left," the man shouted.

"That must be Bob Wilcox," Mommy huffed breathlessly.

Finally, we were on top of the final hill—the same one we coasted down so easily early that morning. Mommy veered, almost recklessly, into the middle of the road.

I followed.

We crossed the double orange lines and turned sharply. The sound of crunching gravel alerted a small huddle waiting in the parking lot. As we careened toward the group, bike club President Pat Gerfin stepped forward, looked at her watch, and announced the time.

"Seven-fifty-eight."

There were no shouts or cheers, like after a home run—just a few pats on the back and some words of congratulations.

Still, I heard something that made me feel like a whole stadium was cheering—it was the wild beating of my own heart.

All I got for riding the Century was an official patch from the League of American Wheelman—and a huge feeling of accomplishment. I still have both.

In 1974 they finally changed the rules, and girls were allowed into Little League. By then I was too old to play, but I could still try out for Babe Ruth Baseball. So I did, was drafted onto an all-boys team, and got to wear a real baseball uniform. (I never did hit that home run.) In high school I played girls' varsity soccer and was captain of the track team.

I still believe that things can change and great things can happen. So, this summer I'm going on a bike ride along Alaska's unpaved Denali Highway. I'll be riding with my daughter.

Alexandra Siy

I grew up near the small town of Clarksville, New York. Our backyard was 100 acres of woods and streams, a place where my husband and I returned to build a home for our own family. My father taught my four brothers and me how to play baseball, instilling in us a lifelong love for the game. But it was my mother who showed me another side to sport—the pursuit of a goal that transcends winning. Discipline, hard work, perseverance, self-reliance, and humility were qualities my mother taught me as we rode our first Century, and several more during my teenage years. These qualities also helped me play team sports in high school, run a marathon in college, ski up and down Mt. Marcy (New York's highest peak), and become a writer. These days I still love bike riding and backcountry skiing.

At a time when young girls were not allowed to play organized sports, my mother gave me the opportunity to challenge myself and achieve something big. Along the way I also gained a deep appreciation for the natural world, realized that "health" food makes you feel better than junk food, and that "unusual" people become your best friends.

I dedicate this story to my mother, Betty Roberts (1927-1985).

On Being Written In

by

Jamie McEwan

Wearing the Landon School for Boys dress-code coats and ties, carrying our uniforms in our brown-and-white plastic gym bags, our team walks into the largest gymnasium I have ever seen.

A high school gym. I am thirteen years old, and I have never been inside a public high school.

It's huge. New. Bare. Clean. In its center lies a blue wrestling mat, reeking with plastic newness, shimmering with white reflections from a battery of lights above.

A high school. Or, as we chanted with derisive elitism at our football games, a "haah" school. "We're gonna beat the haah school."

I am an eighth grader, thirteen years old, and this is my first varsity wrestling match.

I feel proud to be a member of the varsity squad, even though I know that this is largely due to the scarcity of 95-pound wrestlers in our small school. Nevertheless, I will probably earn the first varsity letter in my class. Even "The Big A"—Arthur Smith, the athletic hero of my class ever since five years earlier when he scored the winning touchdown the time we third-graders beat the 65-pound team in the annual Pumpkin Bowl—even The Big A would not earn a varsity letter this year.

My letter would match the varsity letter that my brother, Thomas Edmund McEwan, had earned as an eighth grader, six years before.

Tommy had gone on that year to place second in the Metropolitan D.C. tournament. Later, as a senior, he won the National Prep School Championships.

But in the particular mythos of our family, in the stories told over and over, these accomplishments were not particularly important. It was not degrees, credentials, trophies, position, or money that mattered. What mattered was simply attitude. Spirit.

This pattern had been set by another Thomas Edmund McEwan, our grandfather, a man who grew up in an industrial port town in Scotland. He came to the United States when he was sixteen and spent most of his life working in a yard making refrigerator train cars. Nothing terribly remarkable in all that. No—but picture him at the age of sixteen. Here's the story . . .

His school had been taken over by strangers, the examiners from Edinburgh University. Its own "masters" were reduced to the clerical tasks of handing out and collecting papers. This was the yearly "Bursar's Exam," a test given all over Scotland to select students for coveted full scholarships to the university, a terribly important exam, the climax of their years of schooling.

Grandfather's older brother, Jim, a dignified man a full

fourteen years older than Tom, came by early and found the building quiet, every student hard at work—except for Tom, who was outside in the schoolyard, kicking a soccer ball around.

"Why aren't you working like the rest of them?"

The young Thomas shrugged. "I was finished."

Jim proceeded to quietly berate him for not putting forth his full effort. But when the results were posted two weeks later, Tom and one other student, a girl, were the scholarship winners.

Of course, winning the scholarship is an important part of the story, a necessary element. But the central point was Grandfather's devil-may-care attitude, his insouciance. There was more pride invested in the careless attitude that brought him out to the playground early, and which went along with the family's decision to reject the scholarship and instead send Thomas to America (for even board and books were too much expense for a family of thirteen), than there could possibly be in receiving a college degree.

We were not an old family, nor a distinguished family, but we had our own traditions, our own legends, our own pride. My grandfather's favorite toast, his only toast: "Here's to us. Who's like us? Darned few." He meant it, too. Stories of his fanatic play on the company soccer team—"Mad Dog McEwan" he was dubbed—of his breaking a track record wearing his soccer cleats, of his wit, his willingness to fight, his intellectual superiority, and his lack of ambition, all underlined his peculiar brand of prideful elitism. He was a Scottish Catholic—rare enough in itself—red-haired, blue-eyed, combative, and, toward the young (and toward most of the world, come to think of it), imperturbably condescending. My brother Tom had Grandfather Tom's blue eyes and fair skin. I, like my father, inherited the black hair and dark eyes of my grandmother, a black-Irish O'Donnell by birth.

And so it was that our family did not speak of my brother's wrestling accomplishments except as a kind of background for his crowning achievement: Tom McEwan had never been pinned. Five years of prep school varsity, a year as a post-grad at Andover, more than a hundred matches, and never once pinned. Never pinned. "He's just too . . . too . . ." My father would pause, as if searching for the right word, though he would always come up with the same one: ". . . too cussèd," he would finish with an admiring and prideful smile, a smile that I would have given anything to be able to elicit.

As Landon's entry in the lightest weight class, it is my lot to go first. Feeling exposed and alone, wearing a singlet and tights too binding in the crotch and too baggy below, I walk out under the glaring lights of the high school gymnasium. And coming to meet me is—is—there must be some mistake. This guy, though just my height, has bulging muscles, a thick chest with dark hair that is visible in the scoop of the neck of his singlet. I could swear that he outweighs me by at least twenty pounds. I glance once behind me, hoping to be called back, to be informed of the mistake.

Then I face him, shake his firm hand, step back to my side of the circle. *Remember,* I tell myself, *you don't have to win. You can lose. Winning doesn't matter. As long as you don't . . . get . . .*

It isn't thirty seconds after the starting whistle until I am on my back, blinded by the overhead lights. It cannot happen; it cannot possibly happen. Scissoring my legs, kicking again and again, I try to twist myself onto my stomach. But the weight on my chest seems overwhelming, as if the high school's entire team has piled up on me. I can feel a soft touch on my upper shoulder blade. Desperately wrenching my torso, I lever myself away for a moment. Then comes that touch again, the soft kiss of the yielding mat—impossible!—yet the touch lingers. The slap of the referee's hand on the mat booms beside my ear.

I am released and lie for a moment on my side while the crowd cheers and claps. Then I rise, shake hands once more, and walk unsteadily back to sit beside my teammates.

Dully I watch my teammates lose, one by one. Only our heavyweight wins: one out of the ten of us.

Not that it matters to me. For me, life is over—at least that life I had imagined for myself, had dreamed of, had hoped for. Now, I am forever excluded from the family stories. I am outcast. Whatever the future brings, whatever I accomplish, it is now forever impossible for me to live up to my brother's heroic standard.

After the match, both teams gather on the mat to shake hands yet again, and afterwards we linger to chat. My opponent tells me that he is a senior and that he cut over ten pounds to make weight, then gained most of it back again before the match.

None of this matters. There can be no excuses for me.

"Don't get your feet too close together or cross them," he says helpfully. "You don't have any balance then."

I nod and thank him, though it seems strange to receive advice from the conquering enemy.

Back in the large, clean locker room, we find that one of the parents has left a pan of brownies on the bench for us. I cut myself a large piece and take it to a deserted aisle. Still in my uniform, I sit by myself, eat my brownie, and cry.

Thirteen years old, and my life is over. Done. Finished. All that is left is a ghost, wandering about homeless, without identity, without family. I am no McEwan. McEwans are never pinned.

Four years later I walk into an even larger gym: the Lehigh University gym. All around me are crowds of wrestlers, hundreds of them laughing, talking, sulking, looking tough. There are also scores of coaches, trainers, hangers-on. I envy them. They know someone, they know each other, they have support. I have my father. No one else.

This is the Lehigh Tournament. Also known as the Prep School Nationals.

My coach back at Landon had been skeptical about my even entering the tournament, and he had not expressed the slightest interest in accompanying me to Lehigh, Pennsylvania. No one else on my team had entered; in fact, no one from Landon had entered in six years. The last person to make the trip was my brother. Who had won. Of course.

I didn't blame my coach for lacking faith in me. I had won our local tournament—but just barely. Two matches could have gone either way. In the finals I was behind on points when I caught my overeager opponent off-balance, reversed him, and pinned him.

I stand in line to weigh in. My throat is as dry as a sheet of cardboard. The only thing I have put in my mouth today is a powdered breakfast drink—just the powder. Water, I figure, is too heavy. I am going down a weight class for this tournament, and the last time I was on an accurate scale was almost twenty-four hours ago. I know little about cutting weight and am terrified that I'll be too heavy, and the trip will be wasted.

The weigh-in room is also large, crowded. One weight class at a time, we strip, line up, step on the scale. The guys in the lighter weight classes look terrifically strong to me—and big, bigger than I. And then our turn comes, and my fellow 148-pounders look bigger still, more chiseled, tougher. Intimidating.

When I step onto the balance scale, set at 148, the bar does not budge. Clearly I'm light, well underweight.

"Next."

I'll never know by how much.

"Okay, boy," says my father. "You're in. Let's get you something to eat."

"Drink," I say hoarsely. Pulling on my pants, I head for the water fountain set in the far wall.

My first opponent seems strangely inexperienced to be entered in the Nationals. Despite my nervousness, my feeling that I don't belong here, I win handily.

After that I feel better. I have eaten, and drunk, and won a match. I feel good—until I come up against a tough kid who clearly knows what he's doing. He has not one but *two* coaches shouting from his corner and teammates cheering him on. Will it all end here? But then, there comes a moment in the match, just as he is about to score, that he hangs his head. I throw an arm around it. My other arm is over his back; his left arm is caught between. This is my chance—my only chance.

His right arm is all that supports his weight. I throw my full weight onto him, onto that arm—and the arm folds. Fighting all the way, but with nothing to fight with, he is rolled to his back. He's too strong to mess around with. I have to finish it now.

Within seconds it is over.

That night my father takes me to a movie. It doesn't matter what movie. It's just a chance to sit in the dark for a while, and do nothing, and think nothing.

The next day, while I am sitting on the floor, leaning against a cinderblock wall, waiting for the next round to begin, a kid my age and my size comes to sit beside me.

"Hey, where's Landon School?" he asks.

Now I recognize him: He's the kid I pinned the night before. The tough one. The one who would have beaten me if I hadn't caught him.

"What was your record? . . . Who have you wrestled this year? . . . How about tournaments?" He has lots of questions. He's not unfriendly—but he's not exactly friendly, either. He's almost businesslike.

Then he clears up the mystery. "You know," he says, "I'm out of the tournament unless you win your next match. If you win, I get into the consolation rounds. I can get third."

"Oh. I didn't know it worked like that."

"Yeah. Well, good luck. I think you'll get him."

I'm glad to have someone on my side. For whatever reason.

I do win my next match, and my tough friend wins the consolations, taking third place.

When the consolation rounds are over, the action is moved to a different gym. A single mat is set in the middle of the basketball court. The bleachers are pulled in close around it. The finalists are lined up on opposite sides of the mat, introduced, and called into the center to shake hands.

I'm so flabbergasted by this that, when my turn comes, I don't even notice whose hand I'm shaking.

After the introductions, I decide not to sit in the stands beside my father, and instead wander back behind the bleachers, away from the shouting crowd, away from the matches going on in the lighter weights. And in the half-light behind the bleachers, who do I run into but a kid with a curving scar around one cheekbone. It has been several years, but there's no mistaking him—it's Billy Goldsborough.

"Hi, Jamie. Congratulations on getting in the finals."

"Billy! What are you doing here?"

It turns out that Billy is the manager of one of the wrestling teams. For one school year Billy had lived with our family, but then he had moved away. We had gotten along well during that year, but we hadn't kept in touch. What a strange place to run into him. It feels good to find someone I know.

"Good luck, Jamie. I'll be rooting for you."

When the time comes and my name is called, it feels unnatural and unreal to walk out there alone and shake hands with a stranger—I hadn't even heard of his school!—and stand across the circle from him. Very strange. I feel too nervous to do anything. I feel like an impostor. I don't belong here. I'm not one of these guys.

Luckily, when the match begins, he makes the first move, and I react instinctively, and then it's just wrestling. For a while neither one of us can get the advantage. But then he's clumsy getting back to his feet, and I slide in behind him and lock my arms around his waist. He runs out of bounds, dragging me with him to avoid being taken down.

And when he does that, I realize three things:

One, that *he's* afraid of *me.*

Two, that he's not nearly as good as the tough guy from the quarterfinals.

And three, that I'm going to win.

It's not until the drive back that it really sinks in. Before that, everything—awards, photos, congratulations, a scholarship offer—happens in a kind of haze, a dream state. It's not until the next day, as we thrum along the sun-drenched concrete, my father driving fast but smoothly, that I experience what can best be described as a tremendous relief. Not exhilaration, not triumph—simply relief. I feel light, free, relaxed, as if a burden that I had carried for so long that I had forgotten it was there had suddenly been lifted—the feeling of taking a backpack off at the end of a long day of hiking.

But then, in the midst of this relief, I have a discouraging thought, and the weight settles on me once more.

"You know," I say to my father, "I may have won the tournament. But I can't say that I've never been pinned. Like Tom can. I've been pinned loads of times."

"Yeah, you sure have," chuckles my father. "But that's your style. You've got your own style. Tom was wound up like a spring. Tight! He'd win two to one, four to two. With you, it's crazy, it's a fight to the death, it's pin or be pinned! Every match is like that. On the edge. Do or die! In that second round . . ."

My father goes on to recap the entire tournament, match by match. And in his descriptions, my sloppy pin-or-be-pinned style becomes something gutsy, wild, and somehow admirable. As I listen, I realize that I am hearing a family story being sounded out, tested—a story under construction. For the first time in my life I realize that the family stories are not set in stone. They're invented. They're made up, on the spot, changed, and shifted around and crafted to fit the circumstances. Here I am, being included in the stories, being added in; and all my weaknesses and peculiarities are being transformed into the stuff of legend. Suddenly, even being pinned is a part of the story, a piece of the myth.

And so it happens, that as I listen, the relief becomes complete. The rift is finally healed. I can still be written into the family tradition. I am a McEwan after all.

Jamie McEwan

After graduating from Landon, I attended Yale University, where I majored in English and was captain of the wrestling team. It was during those years that my other sport, whitewater slalom, was included for the first time in the Olympic Games. Emboldened by my successful transformation in wrestling—from perennial loser to national prep champion—I took a full year off from college to concentrate on canoe slalom training. In one year I improved from a seventeenth place in the 1971

World Championships to a third (Bronze Medal) in the 1972 Olympics.

After graduating, I worked in the Yale admissions office and married Sandra Boynton, whom I had met during an acting class my junior year. When Sandra's career as an author/illustrator took off, I returned to international racing, competing in the doubles canoe event with partner Lecky Haller. Whitewater returned to the Olympic program in 1992, and so did I, now a father of four. I placed fourth in the Barcelona Olympics. Retiring from serious competition after 1992, I continued to paddle whitewater rivers around the world, participating in expeditions to Canada, Mexico, Bhutan, and Tibet.

I have published four children's books, and right now I am at work on the great American whitewater novel. Wish me luck.